As Big as a Whale

Adapted by Andrea Posner-Sanchez
from the script "A Whale of a Time" by Chris Nee

Based on the television series created by Chris Nee

Illustrated by Mike Wall

 A GOLDEN BOOK · NEW YORK

Copyright © 2014 Disney Enterprises, Inc. All rights reserved. Published in the United States by Golden Books, an imprint of Random House Children's Books, a division of Random House LLC, 1745 Broadway, New York, NY 10019, and in Canada by Random House of Canada Limited, Toronto. Penguin Random House Companies, in conjunction with Disney Enterprises, Inc. Golden Books, A Golden Book, A Little Golden Book, the G colophon, and the distinctive gold spine are registered trademarks of Random House LLC.

randomhouse.com/kids
ISBN 978-0-7364-3087-6
Printed in the United States of America
10 9 8 7 6 5 4 3 2

Doc McStuffins can't wait to tell her friends about her exciting day. She steps inside her clinic, and her stethoscope glows. Right away, her toys Hallie, Stuffy, Lambie, Chilly, and Hermie come to life.

"I had a great day!" Doc announces to her friends.
"Mom took Donny and me to the aquarium."

Hermie the crab crawls over. "I still remember when
you got me from the aquarium gift shop. . . ."

"The gift shop!" shouts Doc. "I almost forgot—Mom got me a new toy. I'll go get her."

"What kind of toy is it?" asks Stuffy.

"A whale," Doc says as she heads for the door. "I'll be right back."

"How exciting!" cries Hallie. "I don't believe I've ever had the pleasure of meeting a whale."

"Let me tell you, whales are wicked **big**!" Hermie declares.

"Well, then I'd better get the big instruments ready for her 'new toy' checkup," Hallie says as she walks to the back of the clinic.

When Doc returns, she asks everyone to close their eyes. Then she places a tiny beluga whale on the floor.

"Open your eyes now and meet Lula."

Stuffy looks around but doesn't see a whale anywhere. "She's so big she couldn't fit in the door, right?" he asks.

Lambie elbows Stuffy and points down.
"Hi," Lula says in a little voice.

Lula bounces around the room to check out her new home. "This place is really cool," she tells Doc.

Hermie goes to Lula to get a closer look. "A whale smaller than I am?" he whispers a little too loudly. "Wait till the windup toys at the aquarium hear about this!"

Lula hangs her head. "I know, whales aren't supposed to be so small."

"Toys come in all shapes and sizes," Doc says gently.

"Yeah, we weren't even expecting you to be big," Stuffy fibs, to make Lula feel better.

Just then, Hallie arrives. "I got the **biggest** blood-pressure cuff and tongue depressor I could find so we can give our new friend a whale of a checkup."

Stuffy sighs. "Okay, maybe we thought you'd be a *little* bigger."

"I know I'm tiny," Lula admits, "but I will be soooo big someday. I can't wait!"

"I hate to break it to you, but toys don't grow,"
Lambie tells Lula.

Doc picks up the little whale and puts her on
the desk. "Actually, Lula's right," she tells everyone.
"She's a special kind of toy. When we put her in
water, she will grow!"

Doc gives Lula a lift onto a pile of papers. Now she is big enough to read the box she came in.

"See, it says right there that I'm gonna get bigger," Lula says, pointing toward her box. "Can we get started, Doc? I don't want to be the smallest whale anymore."

Hallie brings over a glass of water, and Doc puts Lula inside it.

"Here I grow!" she calls out. Lula closes her eyes and concentrates. A moment later, she leaps out of the glass. "Ta-da!"

The other toys look at each other and shrug.

"Hey, why is everyone still so big?" Lula asks.
"And why am I still small?"

Lambie gives Lula a hug as Doc leans close. "You didn't grow," Doc tells her, "but we love you, big or small."

Doc decides a checkup might explain why Lula
didn't grow in the water. "Let's start by seeing how big
you are now."

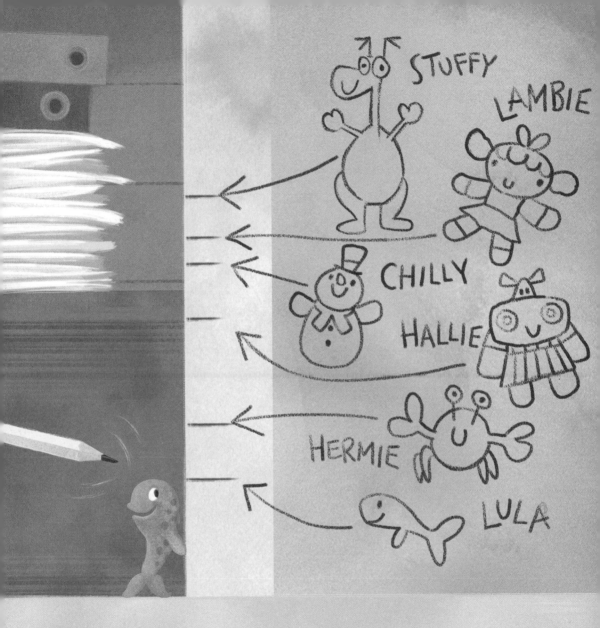

Doc has Lula stand against a wall and uses a pencil to mark her height. Then Doc draws a picture of Lula next to the pencil line.

"Everyone's so much bigger than me," Lula says sadly.

Doc thinks for a moment and then looks at Lula's box. She reads the instructions and comes up with a diagnosis. "You have Wanna-Be-Big syndrome," Doc says. "As much as you want to be big, you just have to wait until your body is ready. The box says you have to spend a couple of hours in water before you can grow."

Lula is ready to do whatever it takes. "I wanna get started now!"

Stuffy helps the little whale back into the glass of water. After a while, she starts to grow! Then she moves into a bigger glass—and grows again!

"I think it's working," says Doc. "Let's do some tests to make sure."

Lula pops out of the glass all by herself and rushes to the height chart. Doc makes a new mark on the wall.

"I'm bigger! I'm bigger!" shouts Lula.

Everyone congratulates her.

But Lula's not done yet. "I was thinking, if I stay in the water overnight, I'll get to be **super-extra big**," she says as she climbs back into the glass.

"We'd better get you something bigger that you can grow into," Doc suggests.

Hallie brings over a pitcher of water and Lula happily jumps right in.

"I'll be back to check on you in the morning," says Doc.

The next morning, Doc goes back to the clinic.
She and the toys head right to the water pitcher.
"It's empty!" Stuffy gasps.
"She's gone!" cries Lambie.

"No, she's not," Doc says in awe, pointing behind them.

Lula is in the fish tank. And she's huge!

"That's a wicked big whale!" shouts Hermie.

Lula leaps out of the tank and gets a hug from Doc. "You look amazing, Lula!" Doc says.

"Being big was definitely worth waiting for," Lula says with a smile. "And I couldn't have done it without you, Doc. I owe you a *big* thanks. Really big!"